WILLOW VALLEY

The Big Bike Race

Tracey Corderoy

Illustrated by Hannah Whitty

For Zöe, thanks for all your help and support. . .

T.C x

First published in the UK in 2012 by Scholastic Children's Books
An imprint of Scholastic Ltd
Euston House, 24 Eversholt Street
London, NW1 1DB, UK
Registered office: Westfield Road, Southam, Warwickshire, CV47 0RA
SCHOLASTIC and associated logos are trademarks and/
or registered trademarks of Scholastic Inc.

Text copyright © Tracey Corderoy, 2012
Illustration copyright © Hannah Whitty, 2012

The rights of Tracey Corderoy and Hannah Whitty to be identified as the
author and illustrator of this work have been asserted by them.

Cover illustration © Hannah Whitty, 2012

ISBN 978 1 407 12476 6

A CIP catalogue record for this book
is available from the British Library.

Printed and bound by CPI Group (UK) Ltd, Croydon, CR0 4YY
Papers used by Scholastic Children's Books
are made from wood grown in sustainable forests.

1 3 5 7 9 10 8 6 4 2

This is a work of fiction. Names, characters, places, incidents
and dialogues are products of the author's imagination or are used
fictitiously. Any resemblance to actual people, living or dead,
events or locales is entirely coincidental.

www.scholastic.co.uk/zone
www.traceycorderoy.com

WILLOW VALLEY

Chapter 1

"Hooray!"

Riley's best friends cheered as he crossed the finish line first. He'd done it! He'd won the running race at his school's Sports Day. *Him!* A little toffee-coloured mouse with sticky-up fur and a twitchy pink nose.

Who would have thought *Riley* could ever win a race against big bouncing bunnies and scurrying squirrels? But Riley had practised and practised for *weeks* and now he had!

As Riley stood panting, his two best friends, Starla and Horatio Spark, hurried up.

"You did it!" cried Starla, throwing her arms in the air. "Well done, Riley! And against *Rothwell* too," she whispered.

"Yeah!" chuckled Horatio. "Serves Rothwell right. Big bully that he is! Well, he won't pick on Riley after *this*!"

The friends glanced over to the thin, slate-grey mouse whose face looked as angry as thunder. He was slumped against a nearby oak tree glowering at Riley.

Columbus, a big, bumbling water vole and Rothwell's only friend, was fanning him with a rhubarb leaf as Rothwell tried to catch his breath.

Suddenly Riley's teacher, Mumford Mole, came pattering up with a winner's rosette, which he handed to Riley. "Goodness!" he beamed. "What a run!

You've beaten the time Rothwell set last year by a whole *three* seconds! You'll go down in Acorns' school history for this!"

"Thanks, Mr Mole!" Riley smiled as Rothwell glared on sourly.

Mumford led them back to the grassy bank where their class was watching the rest of Sports Day. As they passed Rothwell, he gave a small grunt but didn't say anything nasty because their teacher was there. Even so, Riley got the feeling that Horatio was wrong. Rothwell would pick on him even *more* now that he'd beaten him at something. . .

Riley and Starla sat down with their

class. Horatio was in the wheelbarrow race so he had to go. He hurried to the start line, arm-in-arm with little Digby Mole, who was to be his partner in the race.

When they got there, Horatio squatted down on the grass. He had *begged* to be the wheelbarrow and Digby had finally agreed, so the poor little mole had to hold Horatio's big, heavy legs!

Everyone had said it would make more sense for *Digby* to be the wheelbarrow as he was so much lighter. But Horatio Spark never did the sensible thing.

Wheelbarrows, he'd argued, were big, like *him*! And this race called for super-fast scrambling. "After tightrope walking (and eating cake, of course!), *scrambling* is probably my favourite thing!" he'd said.

The whistle blew and they were off! Horatio scrambled for his life, but poor Digby was turning beetroot purple as he tried to hold Horatio's chunky legs.

"I . . . c-can't!" the tiny mole spluttered, as they swayed all over the place. One by one, lighter wheelbarrows scrambled by – *zoom, zoom, zoom*!

Digby and Horatio finished last . . . after a stop at the blackberry bush. Horatio just *couldn't* pass a bush full of berries without gulping down a few. By the time he'd finished, the bush was almost bare!

When he joined Riley on the grass, he had sticky purple juice all over his face and dribbling down his tummy.

Now it was Starla's turn in the acorn-and-spoon race, so she skipped off to the start line. When everyone was ready, the whistle blew and off they all went.

"Come on, Starla!" cheered Horatio and Riley.

They watched as she sped past Bramble Bunny, then Abigail Bright, a chatty red squirrel. Soon Starla was in the lead.

"She's going to win!" Riley cried, his whiskers rippling with excitement. But he spoke just a little bit too soon. . .

Suddenly, Starla tripped over a stone and tumbled on to the grass, her acorn slipping off her shiny spoon.

"*EEEEKKK!*" squealed Horatio. "Pick it up!" But Starla had badly scraped her knee. As the others raced past, Mr Mole helped her up and back to her classmates on the grassy bank.

"Are you OK?" gasped Riley and Horatio.

"Ow," Starla sniffed, looking at her knee. Rothwell, Riley noticed, was now smirking. Why did he have to be so mean? Riley had no idea why Rothwell didn't like him or his friends, but sometimes it was hard to stay cheerful when someone was so horrible.

When Sports Day was over, the three friends headed off to Riley's cave-house for a cool drink. Starla's knee was still very sore, but at least it was the summer holidays now, so there'd be no more school for a whole six weeks, just days of endless playing!

They walked across the village square. Riley and Horatio had a spring in their step but Starla still looked a bit glum.

"Hey, come with me!" said Riley, grinning. He knew just the thing to cheer her up.

He whisked Starla into the baker's shop and bought her the biggest cherry bun he could find. "Thanks," she said, looking quite a bit happier now.

Before they left, they stopped at the noticeboard. Pinned to it was The Big Bike Race poster. The race was taking place in three days' time on the afternoon of the Midsummer's Eve party. A race *and* a party all in one day.

YIPPEE!

Only the children of Willow Valley were allowed to enter the bike race, which happened on Midsummer's Eve every year. It was always a really big event and so much fun.

Crowds would gather to watch the race and there would be popcorn to buy. There'd be ice creams too and bright balloons! And everyone chatted for *weeks* about who might win.

Last year Horatio and Starla had entered. Starla had even come third! She was really very good at riding a bike.

Riley had never taken part. Up until last Christmas he hadn't even owned a

bike. He did now – a shiny red one!
But sadly he still couldn't ride it
properly.

Starla had been giving him lessons
but Riley still fell off a lot and crashed
into bushes and trees! There was no
way he could enter the race this year.
He just wasn't ready. Hopefully though
he would be next year, after a lot more
practice!

Starla used a pencil to cross her name
off the list of riders. "My knee's too sore
for me to race," she sighed. "It really
stings when I bend it and I think all that
pedalling would make it much worse."

"Oooh, never mind!" Horatio said. "I'm not racing this year either. My wheel got bent the other night when I was doing stunts and . . . sort of crashed into the pumpkin patch!" Everybody giggled, even Starla.

They walked on, following the river, which shimmered and shone in the sun.

Three narrowboats sat in a neat line on the cool, clear water. Today the *Kingfisher* was at the front, the *Dragonfly* was at the back and the *Whirligig*, a dark blue boat and the biggest of the three, was gently bobbing about in the middle.

Riley liked these boats very much. They took the animals of Willow Valley on their market trips, which was when they'd sail out into the open countryside to sell their home-made goods. Soon they'd be heading off on their summer trip!

"*Phew,*" panted Riley as they passed the boats. He was so hot. "I really need a drink. Come on!"

When they got to Riley's house, he raced in to show off his winner's rosette. "Whoa!" cried his mum. "Slow down, Mr Patterpaws!"

His sister, who'd been drawing at the table, gave an excited gasp. "Mummy! Look!" cried Mimi-Rose. "Riley's got a ribbon thing!"

Riley's mum gave the toffee bubbling on the stove one final sticky stir. Then she turned to Riley and saw the rosette. "Oh!" she smiled. "You won a race!"

"The running race!" Riley nodded proudly.

Riley breathed in the dreamy smell
dancing on the air. His mum was making
toffee apples for the Midsummer's Eve
party. On the worktop sat a tray of
apples with little willow sticks pushed
into each. Horatio eyed them up, licking
his lips.

Riley poured out some home-made

lemonade and they all gulped it down quickly. As they were finishing, Starla's grandfather arrived to take her home.

"I scraped my knee. Look!" said Starla.

"Dear me," sighed Willoughby White-Whiskers.

"But *I've* been looking after her!" cried Riley quickly.

The old badger nodded and Riley beamed. Willoughby was the wisest badger Riley had *ever* met. When the animals went on market trips, he was the captain of the fleet too! This easily made him Riley's hero.

"Ah," said Willoughby to his

granddaughter, "so *that's* why your name's been crossed off The Big Bike Race list. I saw it just now."

Starla nodded back, looking glum.

"Never mind!" said Willoughby. "At least *Riley's* racing!"

Riley gaped. "M-me?" he stuttered. "But I can't ri—"

"I'll be there!" Willoughby carried on, brightly. "Cheering you all the way! Your name might be last on the list, my lad, but I'm sure that's *not* where you'll finish!"

"My name . . . o-on the list?" said Riley. *He* hadn't written it there! Somebody else must have. But who? And why. . .?

Riley opened his mouth again to tell Mr White-Whiskers that he couldn't do it. That he couldn't even *ride* a bike! But the old badger looked so pleased that his granddaughter's best friend was racing that Riley didn't want to disappoint him.

Riley gulped, thinking hard. He would *have* to race. But could he learn to ride a bike in just *two* days?

Chapter 2

That night Riley dreamt about the bike race. It was a horrid dream! He kept on falling off his bike. *Bump, bump, bump!*

Then Rothwell tied his tail to a bunch of balloons and he floated up into the sky. Higher and higher and higher still! *"Arrggghhh!"*

Suddenly Riley jumped awake, his small black eyes now big and wide and his whiskers all of a quiver. He peered around. It was still quite dark but, thankfully, it was morning.

Riley wandered downstairs and made himself a breakfast of crusty bread spread thickly with blackberry jam, followed by a bowl of nuts and berries. He washed it all down with a mug of cool, creamy milk.

Now the birds outside were chirping bright songs the sunlight was streaming through the window. Riley thought of his mum and Mimi-Rose, still fast asleep in their beds, but he knew he had important things to do.

Sighing, he picked up his bike helmet. Starla and Horatio were coming soon to give him another riding lesson. If *only* he didn't fall off it all the time. . .

As it was now the summer holidays, luckily Riley had the *whole* day to practise. He'd need it too, for now the bike race was the day after tomorrow!

Riley found some paper and a pencil and scribbled a note to his mum. . .

Gone to Mossy Hollow
with Horatio and Starla.
Be back at teatime!
Riley

He left it on the kitchen table, then plodded out into the garden and took his shiny red bike out of the shed.

Riley propped it up against the gate, then waited on the dry stone wall. He watched a fat bumblebee wriggle into a foxglove, looking for a yummy breakfast. The sun was feeling very warm already.

Suddenly, he glimpsed a fluffy-faced badger waving from the bottom of the hill. Beside her was a roly-poly hedgehog eating a huge chunk of cake – probably his *third* breakfast! Starla and Horatio were here. . .

Riley scrambled off the wall, popped on his helmet and wheeled his bike down the hill to meet them. "Let's go to

Mossy Hollow!" he said.

"Good idea," Starla nodded. No one
would disturb them there.

"Don't worry, Riley!" Horatio burped.
"You'll soon be great at riding that bike!"

"I hope so," Riley muttered under
his breath.

They set off along the riverbank, where a clump of feathery willow trees dipped their branches into the river.

Next, they passed the narrowboats bobbing about on the water. Then on they went through the pretty village square. Beyond this was another hill leading up into Bluebell Wood. They climbed the hill past Starla's cave-house, then stopped in the wood for a little rest in the cool sea of bluebells.

Finally, they carried on through the wood, which led them out into a small cove surrounded by craggy cliffs. "Mossy Hollow!" Starla smiled. They'd arrived.

Mossy Hollow was as quiet as ever. Hardly anyone ever came here. It was the perfect place for picnics, for playing knights and dragons, *and* for learning to ride a bike in secret.

Riley looked around for a good spot to ride. There were steep, rocky cliffs on three sides. He'd stay away from them! There were also big, mossy boulders that stuck up out of the grass. Riley knew he'd have to be very careful.

He chose his spot, jumped on his bike and *"Eeek!"* he was off – swerving and wobbling and skidding through the moss!

"*Whoa!*" gasped Riley, just missing a rock. *Why* couldn't he just ride straight! He was going to fall off . . . any minute now. He was!

Riley tried pedalling harder. He was hoping that going faster might help. It didn't. In fact, it only made things worse.

"Riley!" cried Starla suddenly. "Watch out for those nettles!" She peeped through her trembling paws. "And the boulders!"

"*What?*" shouted Riley, looking over at her.

"*Look straight ahead!*" cried Starla. "You have to watch where you're *going*!"

Riley looked ahead. *"Uh oh!"* he squeaked. He was heading right for a big, mossy boulder.

"Pull the brakes!" Horatio yelled. So Riley quickly tugged them with all his might. . .

EEEEEEEEEE! the brakes squealed noisily. But it was too late. "*Help!*" gulped Riley as the boulder came closer. Closer and closer, *until. . .*

CRASH!

Riley's wheel had smacked right into it and he was thrown off his bike into the air.

"Oh no!" gasped Starla as he tumbled back down. *"Nettles!"* she shouted. "Big ones!"

Riley saw the nettles but it was no good. He was heading straight for the middle. *"Yow!"* he howled as he landed nose first. "Eeeee . . . ooooo . . . ouuuchh!"

"Here!" puffed Starla, racing over with the biggest dock leaf she could find. Riley took it and patted his throbbing nose as Horatio wheeled his bike across.

"It's no good. I'm rubbish," Riley sighed, shaking his head.

"*Ha ha!*" sniggered a sudden voice from behind. "That's *just* what I was saying!"

The friends spun round to see Rothwell and Columbus laughing.

Rothwell had his racing bike with him. It was black and silver and it gleamed in the sun. Riley had often seen him on it, doing wheelies and showing off.

Rothwell had always been *brilliant* at riding a bike.

"It's going to be *great*," Rothwell smirked, "when *I* speed past *you* in The Big Bike Race, Riley! Won't break any records *that* day, will you?"

"Unless he breaks the one for the *wobbliest* rider!" snorted big bumbling Columbus.

"*I* make the jokes around here!" snapped Rothwell.

"Ooo – sorry" blushed Columbus.

Riley thought for a moment. So . . . it had been him! *Rothwell* must have written his name on that list and entered him into The Big Bike Race. He wanted to get him back for Sports Day, and Rothwell *knew* that he could win this race quite easily!

Rothwell jumped on his bike and sped away, leaving everyone – including Columbus – in a swirling blizzard of dust. The coughing water vole lumbered off after him.

"Bully!" Horatio called after Rothwell. "Don't you worry, Riley."

But Riley was very worried indeed.

Chapter 3

Riley practised for the rest of the morning but his riding didn't get any better. He crashed into big things (and small things too!). And he wobbled and fell off, over and over again.

They stopped to have lunch but to Horatio's horror, he realized they hadn't brought any food! "What are we going to *do*?" he wailed. "I'll starve!"

Starla looked around. There was an ancient apple tree groaning with big, juicy apples. Now, which one of them should climb it, she wondered? Not her, as her knee still stung when she bent it.

"Oooo, I'll do it!" Horatio cried, but Starla shook her head. The last time *Horatio* had climbed a tree, he'd got stuck for *hours*!

"Let Riley climb up instead," she said. "He can shake the apples down and we can both catch them."

"OK!" cried Horatio. That sounded like fun!

So Riley climbed up the tree and in no time at all, a big pile of apples sat on the ground and everyone tucked in.

Afterwards, Riley got back on his bike,
but his riding seemed worse than before!
He swerved and he skidded. He kept
falling off and bruising his little knees.
"That's it!" he scowled at last. "I'm
going home!"

His nose still stung after his fall in the
nettles and he kept on imagining Rothwell's
face when Riley came last in the race.

He felt like marching straight back
to that noticeboard and crossing his

name off the race list! But that would disappoint Mr White-Whiskers, who had said he was going to cheer for him. And his mum and Mimi-Rose were so excited for him, too. No, he had to go through with the race. He *had* to.

The friends trooped back to Riley's cave-house with very long faces. When they arrived, Riley's mum was sewing bunting for the Midsummer's Eve party. The toffee apples were all ready now.

"Oh Riley!" gasped Mimi-Rose as they trudged in through the door. "Did you fall off your bike again?" She pointed to the bruises on his knees and the nettle stings on his nose. Riley nodded and Horatio and Starla both sighed.

"Oh dear!" said his mum, putting down her needle. She quickly found some witch hazel and dabbed it on Riley's knees. Then she sat them all down at the kitchen table with a comforting glass of elderflower cordial.

Horatio gazed at the toffee apples sitting on a big tray but Starla's eyes were drawn to the colourful bunting.

"Oooh, I can't *wait* for the party!" she cried. Hoot Hill Barn, where it was always held, was going to look prettier than ever!

Riley sighed. *Normally* he'd be excited too. But he had to get through The Big Bike Race first this year. . .

"Fancy a toffee apple?" asked his mum, with a smile.

"Really?" Riley's ears pricked up. "But those are for the party."

"Well, I'm *so* proud of you!" his mum replied. "Learning to ride a bike isn't easy, but you're trying so hard."

"And me!" cried Horatio suddenly. "I've been *helping* hard too!" He tried to look his very hungriest as he gazed up at her hopefully.

"Oh all right!" laughed Riley's mum.

"You can *all* have one!"

"Even *me*?" squeaked Mimi-Rose.

"Yes, even you!"

She handed them out and the room turned silent as everyone tucked in.

Riley's toffee apple tasted so good – like a shiny, round bundle of his *favourite* things! Like leaping through the swaying corn. Like playing hide-and-seek in the rain. Like starry nights munching toast by the fire. Like sleepovers with his friends. . .

Before they went home, Horatio and Starla promised they'd come back tomorrow. They'd take his bike to Bluebell Wood where it was nice and shady. "We'll get you riding that bike properly no matter what!" said Starla.

"Leave it to us!" nodded Horatio, beaming.

As Riley waved goodbye to them, he felt a little bit better. Starla and Horatio were always there when he needed them.

The next morning, Riley was up again before anyone else. He scurried downstairs, had some bread and honey and a cool mug of milk. Then he left another note for his mum on the table. . .

Gone to Bluebell Wood
with Horatio and Starla.
I am going to learn to ride that bike.
I AM!

Grabbing his helmet, Riley hurried
outside. Horatio and Starla were coming
through the gate.

"Ready?" smiled Horatio "I am – *look*!"
He heaved up a heavy picnic basket
crammed with his favourite goodies.

"No apples for us today!" he
chuckled. "I've got ginger cake and
ginger pop and gingerbread men too!"

"Thanks, Horatio!" said Riley with
a grin.

"I've been thinking too," said Starla.
"When *I* need to learn something new,
I always use books to help me. So I
thought we could go to Library Cave

on the way to Bluebell Wood and find a book about learning to ride a bike!"

Riley thought about this. "OK!" he squeaked. "Let's go!"

He got his bike out of the shed and wheeled it off down the hill as his friends walked beside him. Everyone seemed a lot brighter today.

Library Cave had only just opened by the time they arrived. Riley left his bike and helmet outside and they all went in.

The heavy stone shelves were filled with books. Everyone searched through the books about bikes, and very soon Starla had found the perfect one.

The book was called *No More Falling Off Your Bike!* *(But have some plasters just in case. . .)* "This book's just right!" Starla beamed.

"Yep," nodded Riley.

They got the book stamped, grabbed Riley's bike, then dashed off to Bluebell Wood. The wood was cool and filled with bluebells, which Riley thought would make a nice soft landing!

Before Riley started practising he flicked through the book. It was really very useful! It showed you how to ride straight, how to signal and turn, how to start and stop (without crashing into things!), and how to look after your bike properly.

It also told you all about gears. "Oh!" gasped Riley, reading down the page. "No *wonder* I've been finding it hard. My bike's been in *uphill* gear when I haven't been going uphill! Maybe that's why I've been wobbling all the time!"

Riley clicked his gears into *normal*, then popping on his helmet, he set off along the track. He was still quite wobbly but not as bad as yesterday, and his bike felt so much smoother to ride now.

Riley practised stopping next. Horatio lined up a row of fir cones and Riley had to stop before he hit them. "Pretend they're squirrels!" Horatio chuckled. "A row of Abigail Brights!"

He quickly gave them each a frilly fern tail, some little pebble eyes and a few long bluebell leaves for whiskers. Then Riley tried his best not to squash them flat!

After this, Riley practised riding straight, riding round tree stumps, riding fast and slow. Then, finally, he had a go at signalling.

Although he was better at most things now, Riley couldn't get the hang of

signalling. Every time he took a paw off
the handlebars he would wobble and
nearly crash.

"I know what you need!" Horatio cried.

"What?" said Riley.

"Lunch!"

They stopped to eat. Riley felt pleased. He was riding *so* much better now and lunch looked great today. In fact, everything about *today* was so much better than yesterday!

Everyone chatted happily as they nibbled gingerbread men. Then they drank ginger pop until they couldn't stop hiccupping!

"I just have to do *(hic!)* my best," said Riley, "in the race tomorrow."

"*(Hic!)* Yeah!" grinned Horatio. "You don't have to win! Also *(hic!)*, I'm making something special to bring with me tomorrow."

"And I'll be there *(hic!)* with Grandpa!" smiled Starla. "Cheering *(hic!)* you right to the end!"

"Thanks! *(Hic!)*" said Riley with a grin.

After a little more practice, they walked home together, the book tucked safely under Riley's arm. He'd read it again at bedtime, he decided. He didn't need to *win* the race. He just needed to do his best. . .

Chapter 4

The day of The Big Bike Race arrived. That meant the Midsummer's Eve party too. Everyone in Willow Valley loved this day! The race was always so exciting and the party afterwards in Hoot Hill Barn would go on until the moon and stars shone bright!

The smell of baking filled the air when Riley came down for breakfast. His mum was checking her party list of things still to do.

First, her tarts would need filling with blackberries while her scones cooked. Then lots and lots of cream would need to be whipped. Finally, she'd need to go strawberry-picking outside in the garden, before cheering Riley on in The Big Bike Race!

"Good morning, Riley!" she said brightly. "How are you feeling today?"

"I'm OK," murmered Riley. But really he felt quite nervous about the race.

Suddenly, they heard the tiny patter of feet and Mimi-Rose scurried in. "Porridge time!" she cried, climbing up on to her chair.

When it was ready, she wolfed hers down, but Riley ate much more slowly. His tummy felt a little bit whirly-pop today!

When he had finally finished, he went outside to polish his bike. The race wasn't starting until two o'clock, so he had lots of time. Even if he didn't win today, he wanted his bike to look its very best.

The morning passed quickly and before Riley knew it, his mum was serving up lunch! Horatio and Starla would be coming soon to walk with him to the race.

Riley still didn't feel much like eating, but he knew he'd need his strength for later. So he nibbled on a crust of freshly baked bread. Then he had a few chunks of cheese. To finish, as a treat, his mum gave him some rings of sweet dried apple, along with a big mug of creamy milk, his favourite!

No sooner had he finished than his friends arrived and they set off to the race. His mum and Mimi-Rose would follow a little later.

The race was to start at Buttonoak Mill, then loop around part of the valley. "I don't want to get there too soon," said Riley, feeling even more nervous now.

"We won't," smiled Starla kindly. "Don't worry."

They walked down the hill, Riley pushing his bike, which sparkled in the sun.

"You don't have to worry about anything!" said Horatio, as they crossed the old crooked stone bridge. "I've made you a stretcher, see?"

He tapped the thing stuffed under his arm. Riley had wondered what it was. It looked like two tatty old tent poles with a bed sheet wrapped around them. "So if you fall off your bike," said Horatio, "we can carry you back home!"

"Thanks!" gulped Riley.

"Just remember all the things in your bike book!" said Starla.

"Er," muttered Riley, scratching his head, "I'm trying!"

They walked along, through meadows and fields, Riley thinking all the way. Starting . . . stopping . . . signalling *(eek!)*, cycling nice and straight. There was such an *awful* lot to remember!

When they arrived at Buttonoak Mill, a busy blur of colour met their eyes. Riley stopped and his small pink nose twitched nervously, butterflies now dancing in his tummy.

The place was packed with riders and bikes in all the colours of the rainbow! Abigail Bright's bike was a fizzy lime green with a daisy-chain wound around the handlebars.

Bramble Bunny's was light blue with a basketful of carrots strapped to the front. He'd nibble them as he raced along, no doubt!

Digby Mole's bike was a deep custard yellow. He was riding it round and round in circles as if he couldn't *see* straight! It made Riley feel quite dizzy just to watch!

Little Phoebe Badger had a pale lilac bike, the colour of clouds at sunset.

Shooting from the ends of its handlebars were little bunches of streamers, which made it look like it had sprouted hair!

And there was Rothwell, standing beside his shiny black racing bike. It had a snazzy silver bell, big flashy mudguards and more gears than anyone else's. It looked like it might go *very* fast. . .

Columbus was fussing round Rothwell's bike, busily polishing everything. Suddenly, Rothwell caught Riley's eye and smirked.

There were also squirrels selling popcorn, the smell of which danced on the air. And hedgehogs were holding huge bunches of balloons to sell to the excited crowd, trying their best not to pop them on their sharp prickles!

The crowd that lined the racetrack were chatting excitedly, placing bets on who might win. Starla spotted her grandfather over at the start line, giving his eager race-helpers some final instructions.

Hector Rabbit was holding a clipboard and Benjamin Bobtail had a small silver whistle. They nodded their heads, their long ears flapping as Willoughby spoke to them.

Suddenly, Benjamin pipped his whistle and the crowd went very quiet. "Racers to the start line, please!" called Willoughby, giving Riley a little smile. Riley gave a gulp. This was it!

"Good luck!" whispered Starla as Horatio thrust the stretcher into the air.

"Surprise!" he cried, as it quickly unfolded.

"Oh!" squeaked Riley, his eyes suddenly wide.

The stretcher, it seemed, wasn't *only* a stretcher but a good luck banner too! On the sheet wrapped around the tent poles Horatio had scribbled a message. . .

However badly Riley rides today, he's still the BEST friend EVER!

Riley managed a little smile. Then he plodded off to the start line, pushing his bike beside him as Rothwell quickly zoomed past on his.

When everyone was gathered, Hector Rabbit tested all the brakes and bells. Then he checked all the helmets too. "All fine!" he called, making lots of little ticks on his clipboard.

"Jolly good!" smiled Willoughby White-Whiskers. "Now then, everyone, on the count of three, Benjamin Bobtail will blow his whistle and this year's Big Bike Race will begin!" Benjamin put the whistle to his lips and waited.

"Just follow the arrows on the trees," nodded Willoughby. "The first one back will be the winner!"

"And the *last* one back," muttered Rothwell, "will be Riley!"

Mr White-Whiskers raised a green flag. "One. . ." he called and Riley squeaked.

"Two. . ." and Riley shivered.

"*Three!*"

Benjamin blew his whistle and Riley heard Starla shout, "GO!"

Rothwell had already shot away in a cloud of swirling dust. Everyone else had trundled off too, even little Phoebe Badger!

With a nervous gulp, Riley started to pedal and wobbled off after the others. "Go, Riley!" cheered Starla.

"Go *faster*!" shouted Horatio.

"Oh wait!" squeaked Riley, remembering his gears. He chose the right one for riding on the flat and began to ride steadier at once.

"Fa – er!" Horatio mumbled, through a mouthful of popcorn.

Riley followed the orange arrows on the trees as the other riders sped off. They led away from Buttonoak Mill down a dusty track, then up a steep hill into the leafy lanes of Willow Valley.

The shouts of the crowd began to fade as Riley puffed uphill, the other riders already on the other side.

He might have not crashed his bike yet – or even tumbled off – but, right now, he was well and truly *last*!

Chapter 5

Riley rode on past Stumpy's Stile, then through a sunny field of poppies, carefully following the arrows on the trees.

Sometimes they took him through shady woods. Sometimes through grassy meadows. And once through a field of cows with breath like tornados!

He was riding so much better now than he had at the start of the week. This was mostly thanks to Starla and Horatio, who had helped him so much.

Riley thought that it would be really nice if he didn't finish last. A lovely way to thank them for all their help.

"No," he said, with a little sigh. He'd never catch the others now! Anyway, Starla and Horatio wouldn't mind *where* he finished in the race. Like they'd said, he just needed to do his best. . .

Riley followed the arrows through Ten Oaks Field. He was riding quite fast now! He felt the wind blowing back his whiskers.

He cycled on down the lanes, going faster and faster and faster. Learning about gears had been the best thing ever!

Riley sped on through Buttercup
Meadow, then down a bumpy track
which led around the allotments.
Podrick, a rather grumpy old hare, was
digging up his potatoes. He raised his
spade and even smiled as Riley cycled
by. "Go on, that's the way!" he called.
"You're nearly catching the others!"

"W-what?" muttered Riley. Had he heard right? He was near to the rest of the riders? Wow – he must have being going faster than he'd thought!

"Thanks, Mr Hare!" Riley cried, waving him goodbye. Then Riley realized what he'd just done. He'd taken a paw off the handlebars! He could *even* ride with one paw now! He couldn't *wait* to show Starla and Horatio!

Riley sped off down the lane, pedalling with all his might. Then suddenly, as he rounded a bend, he spotted the back of lots of little heads just a little way ahead. It was the other riders, with Rothwell at the front. But Riley was getting closer and closer all the time!

"Come on!" he squeaked to himself as the riders disappeared over the final hill. It wasn't far to the finish line now.

Riley popped his bike into *uphill* gear and hurried up the hill too. "Wheee!" he cried as he flew down the other side.

He could see the other riders again and he wasn't far behind! They rounded a bend and Riley did too. But wait. Riley gasped. *What was that?*

Riley's tyres screeched to a halt.

Columbus was lying at the side of the lane, gripping his leg and sobbing loudly. Great fat tears were rolling down his cheeks as he rocked back and forth, howling.

Quickly, Riley leapt off his bike and hurried over to him. "Columbus!" he cried breathlessly. "What have you done?"

Columbus gave a big, snotty sniff, then looked down at his leg. A nasty purple lump was popping up.

"R-Rothwell," he sniffed. "His m-mudguard bashed me as I stepped out t-to cheer him on."

His bottom lip began to quiver as he gazed down at the lump. "It r-really, really hurts!" Columbus blubbered.

"But didn't he *stop*?" Riley said. "Didn't Rothwell stop to help you?"

Columbus shook his sorry head. "No."

"But you're meant to be his best friend!" cried Riley. "I'd always stop for *my* friends if *they* were hurt."

Riley looked along the lane and Columbus did too. "You can still c-catch them!" Columbus sniffed. "I think Rothwell's tyre might have punctured when he hit me. You m-might even win the race if you hurry. Go on!"

Riley's eyes shot to his bike. But then back to Columbus. "No," he said. "I'm not leaving you here. That leg looks really sore. Come on, I'll help you back to the finish line!"

Riley helped Columbus on to his bike, then walked behind it, slowly pushing him back. When they reached the crowd, Horatio and Starla ran up.

Riley could see Rothwell at the
finish line, taking the winner's cup
from Mr White-Whiskers. "Riley, what
happened?" panted Horatio. He pointed
at Columbus. "And why have you got
him on your bike?"

"I'll tell you later," whispered Riley as

Columbus's lip started quivering again. "Let's get him on to the stretcher. He's hurt his leg."

They helped Columbus off the bike and on to the wonky stretcher. He looked very sorry for himself now.

"Look, Riley!" said Starla, suddenly. "Grandpa's coming to see you."

"Oh!" said Riley, wondering what Mr White-Whiskers might say. He hoped he wouldn't be *too* disappointed that Riley had finished last in the race.

Willoughby White-Whiskers wandered over. "I know I came last!" Riley cried. "But I did try my best, I promise!"

"No one can ask any more than that!" smiled Willoughby.

"But he *did* do more! *He did!*" came a voice. It was Columbus, whose watery eyes gazed up at Mr White-Whiskers. "Riley stopped to help me!" he cried.

Willoughby White-Whiskers turned to Riley. "Is this true?" he asked him.

"Err . . . yes!" Riley replied. "I couldn't just leave him lying in the lane. He was hurt."

The wise old badger nodded slowly, thinking very hard. "I see," he said finally. "And are you coming to the party tonight?"

"Oh yes!" squeaked Riley happily. The race was finally over and done with. Now it was party time!

With that, Riley's mum and Mimi-Rose appeared. "Riley!" squealed his little sister as his mum gave him a hug, "I made a ribbon-thing for you!" And she stuck a big *Good Try!* rosette on his helmet.

"Right then, Riley!" said his mum.
"Let's get you home and washed. We've
got a party to go to!"

"Wait!" cried Starla. "I'll ask my mum
if I can come to your house too. I can
help carry the food to the party."

"Oooh, me too!" Horatio cried. "Bagsy
I carry the toffee apples!"

"But you'd eat them all!" cried everybody, laughing.

Horatio and Starla asked their parents, who said that they could go. But first they needed to make sure Columbus was OK.

Riley's mum took his bike and began walking home with Mimi-Rose, while Riley and his friends headed off to the first aid tent with Columbus.

Just before they got there, Rothwell zoomed up on his bike. "Hey, look here Columbus!" he cried, waving his cup about smugly. "Big Bike Race Winner! Um, that would be *me!*"

Nobody spoke. Rothwell might have won the race, but nobody wanted to celebrate with him. Not after he'd left his best friend hurt in the lane.

"Coming to the party, then?" Rothwell asked Columbus. "I'll call for you at five!"

"No," said Columbus quietly. "I'd rather . . . rather," he swallowed hard. "I'd really much rather go by myself tonight."

Rothwell gaped. He narrowed his eyes and glowered at them all. "Suit yourself!" he muttered to Columbus.

With that, Rothwell sped away,

leaving everyone in a cloud of dust. When it had cleared, Riley looked at Columbus.

"It's OK," he said to him. "You can play with us at the party!"

"Really?" said Columbus.

"Yes," smiled Riley. And it was very nearly time!

Chapter 6

When Riley got home he had a quick wash then he and his friends played leapfrog in the garden. No one would leap over Horatio, though, because of his sharp prickles!

The Midsummer's Eve party in Hoot Hill Barn would be starting at five o'clock, so everyone set off just after four-thirty.

Riley's mum had given each of them some party food to carry and four little tummies rumbled loudly as they marched along.

Riley held the tray of toffee apples, which glinted in the sun. "I'm starving!" he cried.

"Me too!" squeaked Mimi-Rose.

She had a basket of strawberries, all big and red and juicy! When no one was looking, she'd swipe one and cram it into her mouth. Soon, sticky juice dribbled down her fluffy white chin.

Starla carried the blackberry tarts but Horatio was given the bunting, as he wouldn't be tempted to eat this!

Riley's mum held the scones, which had been covered with a red and white cloth to stop gangs of greedy little bugs helping themselves!

They hurried down the hill, then walked beside the river. Twinkles of sunlight danced on the water like little shooting stars and the air was filled with the smell of wild garlic growing on the hillsides.

They strolled on past the narrowboats, which glimmered in the sun. Then they wandered through the pretty village square.

Hoot Hill Barn was up the next hill

behind the little shops. As they climbed uphill, the sweet smell of woodsmoke drifted down to meet them. Old Podrick must have lit a fire to cook the sausages!

At the top of the hill, the barn doors were open. Three tables had been covered with white linen cloths ready for the party food. They found some space on one and unloaded their goodies.

"Mum," said Riley, excitedly, "can *I* put up the bunting? Horatio and Starla can help me too!"

"Oh go on then!" smiled his mum.

So Riley and the others raced outside and hung the bunting on the fence.

As they did, streams of animals came pouring up the hill, laden with heavy baskets of food. "Oh look!" cried Riley. "The moles have brought pasties. Yum!"

When all the food had been unpacked and everyone was gathered in the barn, Willoughby White-Whiskers stood up on a hay bale.

He beamed down at the excited crowd, all eager to eat and dance. "Let the party begin!" he cried.

"Hooray!" cheered everyone.

With that, a stampede of tiny paws pattered to the tables, and plates were quickly piled high with food.

Little Phoebe Badger had *three* blackberry tarts and Digby Mole had a toffee apple almost as big as his head! Horatio, as always, had a bit of everything on *his* plate!

There were hay bales dotted around the barn on which they sat to eat. Riley and his friends grabbed one near the tables to be close to the food for Horatio. Rothwell, though, was sitting near the door with his mum and dad. He usually had Columbus with him, but not tonight. . .

Columbus was sitting with his own family, tucking into sausages in buns. Riley waved and he waved back.

"Come over later and we'll play!" called Horatio, and the big bumbling water vole nodded back, grinning.

"Mmmm," said Starla dreamily, biting into a fairy cake. It was lemon-flavoured with a cream cheese frosting and was decorated with sugar-paste pansies. "The rabbits do make the best cakes *ever*!" she smiled.

Riley wolfed down two delicious pasties, followed by a huge cream puff. "Yum!" he breathed as big blobs of cream sat on his whiskers like snowballs. This was the best Midsummer's Eve party he could ever remember. And everyone ate and ate until they were full!

After the food, came the dancing.
Mumford had brought his fiddle and
Willoughby had his old tin whistle.
Between them they struck up a jolly tune,
and in no time at all everyone was dancing.
"Wheee!" cried Starla, swinging Riley
around as Horatio tapdanced beside them.

"Faster!" giggled Riley. "Faster, faster!"

Eventually, they got too hot so popped back to the tables for a drink. While they were there, Columbus appeared.

"Would you like to play hide-and-seek?" he asked. "My leg's better now!"

"I would!" smiled Starla.

"Me too!" nodded Riley

"Let's go outside!" Horatio cried. "Come on!"

They gulped down their drinks and raced out to the field, where they played hide-and-seek for ages. Then they played tag. Then stuck-in-the mud. It was so much fun!

When, at last, they stopped for a rest, the big orange sun had slipped over the hill and a silver moon hung in the sky. Tiny stars were beginning to twinkle and moths danced over their heads. This was one day Riley would never forget!

They wandered back in, arm-in-arm. The dancing had stopped and everyone was sitting down, chatting.

Pretty lanterns hung down from the beams, casting soft shadows on the walls, and everything looked very warm and cosy.

Willoughby White-Whiskers got to his feet. The party was about to end.

"Thank you all for coming!" he said. "It's been a wonderful party! But, before you go, I have a medal to award, following the bike race today."

Rothwell's ears pricked up at once as he sat on his hay bale. A medal? That must be for him! He was the winner of the race, after all.

Willoughby looked around the crowd, from one head to another. "Ah," he said finally, pointing a paw. "There he is!"

Starla nudged Riley. Horatio nudged Riley. Willoughby was pointing at *him*! Slowly, Riley got to his feet and edged through the crowd to Mr White-Whiskers.

"For you!" said Willoughby, hanging the medal around Riley's neck.

"B-but. . ." stuttered Riley. He'd come *last* in the race. Why was *he* getting a medal?

"Today," Mr White-Whiskers said to the crowd, "Riley did something very kind. Very kind and very brave too. During the race he stopped to help someone. Someone who was hurt. And because of that, he came last – even though he knew he'd be teased for it. In doing so, he showed that friendship is to be prized above being crowned winner. That it is *how* you race the race that really matters."

Suddenly everyone was clapping. All except Rothwell. He was glowering at Riley, who, right now, didn't care!

That night, as Riley wandered home, he felt about ten feet tall. "Thanks," he said to Starla and Horatio, "for teaching me to ride my bike. Without you, I'd still be falling off!"

"Let's go bike-riding tomorrow!" said Starla, whose knee now felt much better.

"But my *wheel*!" sighed Horatio. "It's bent, remember?"

Riley thought. "We'll straighten it!" he cried. "We'll *sit* on it, all together!"

"That should do the trick!" Horatio chuckled.

3

Then the three best friends skipped off home as the bright moon lit their way. They would meet up early in the morning and sort out Horatio's bike. Then they'd ride and ride and ride together, *all day. . .*